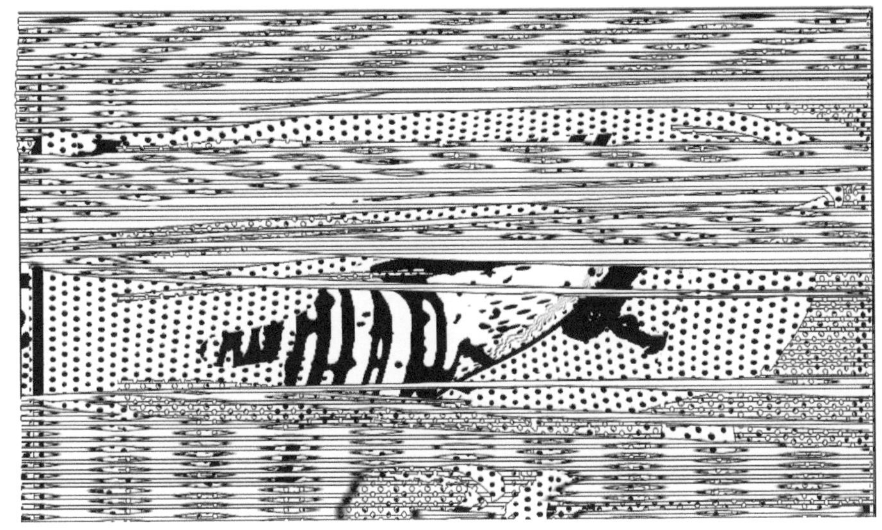

and yet...

by Rosaire Appel

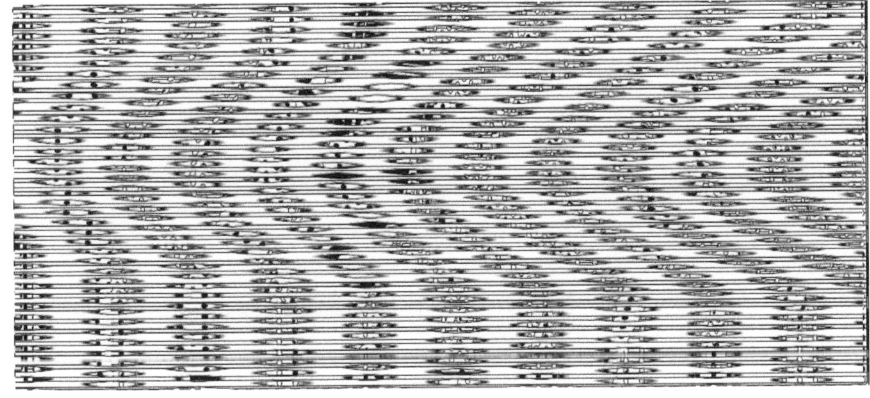

PRESS RAPPEL

ISBN: 978-1-105-57228-9

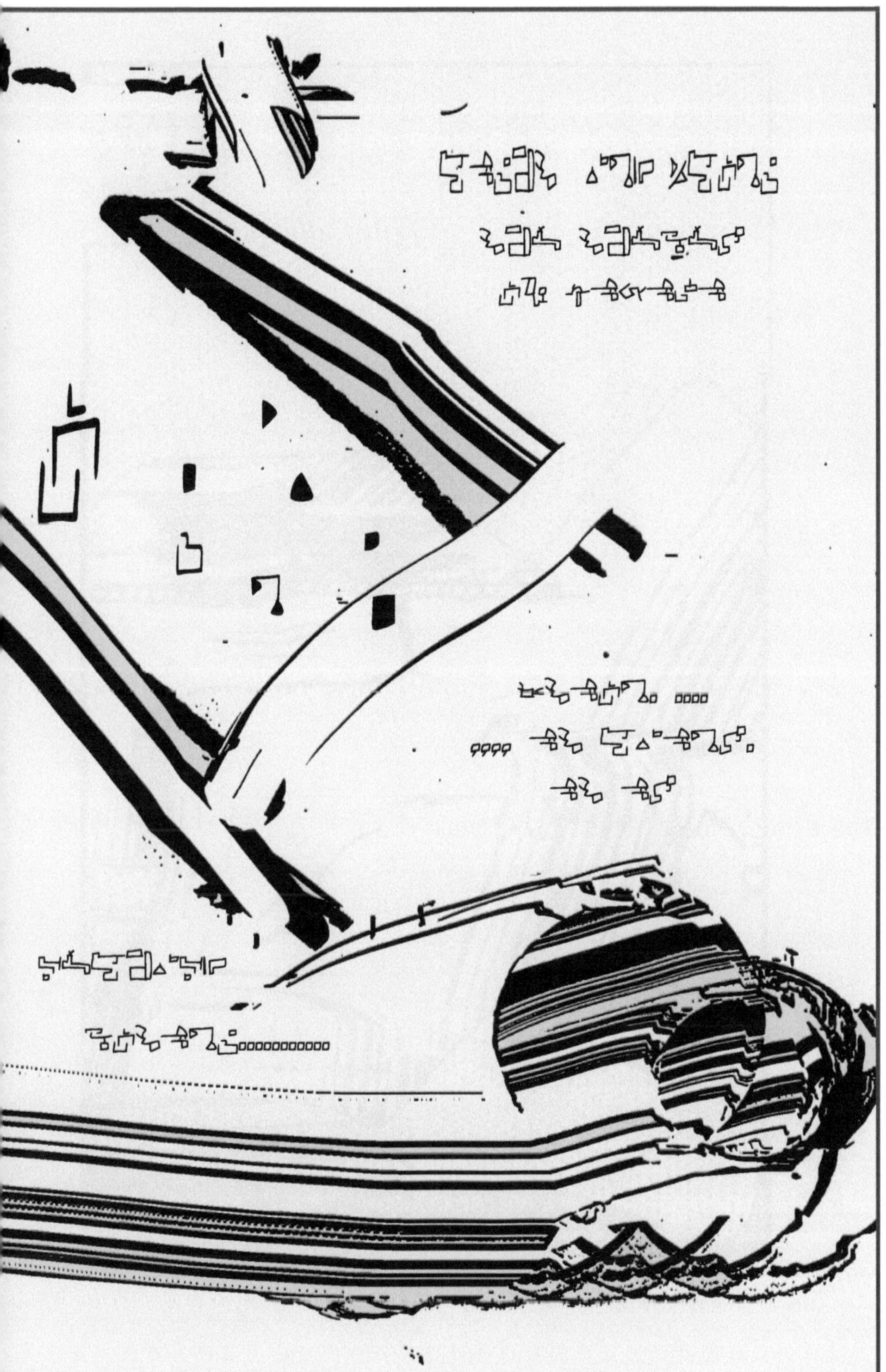

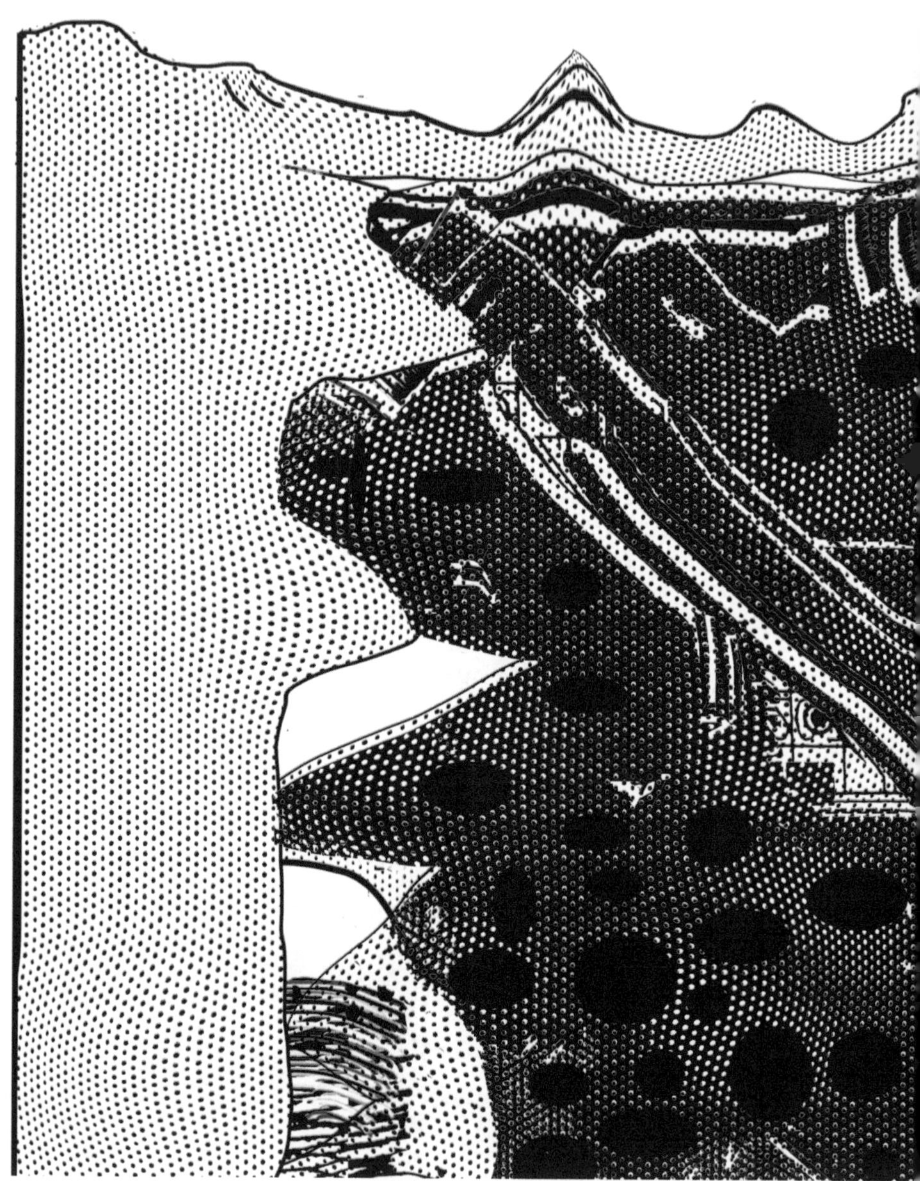

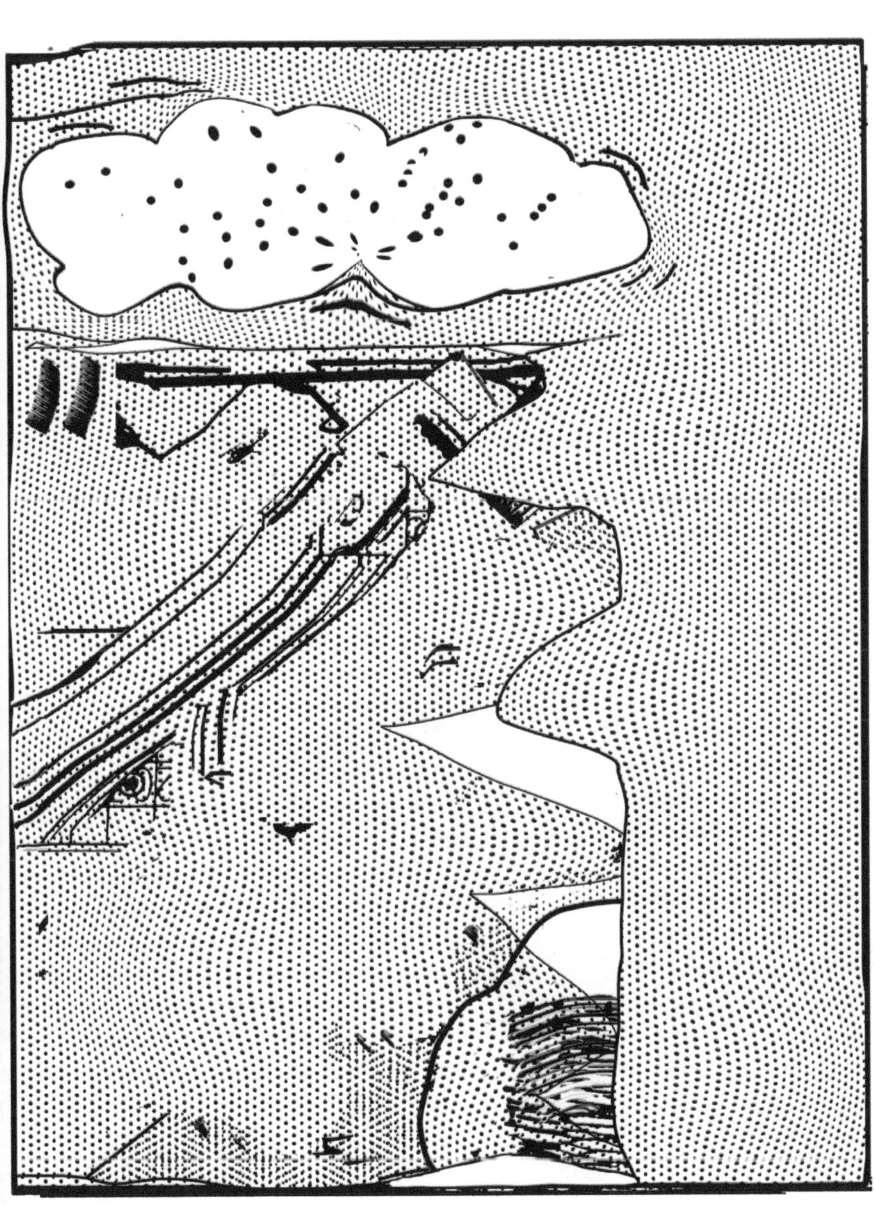

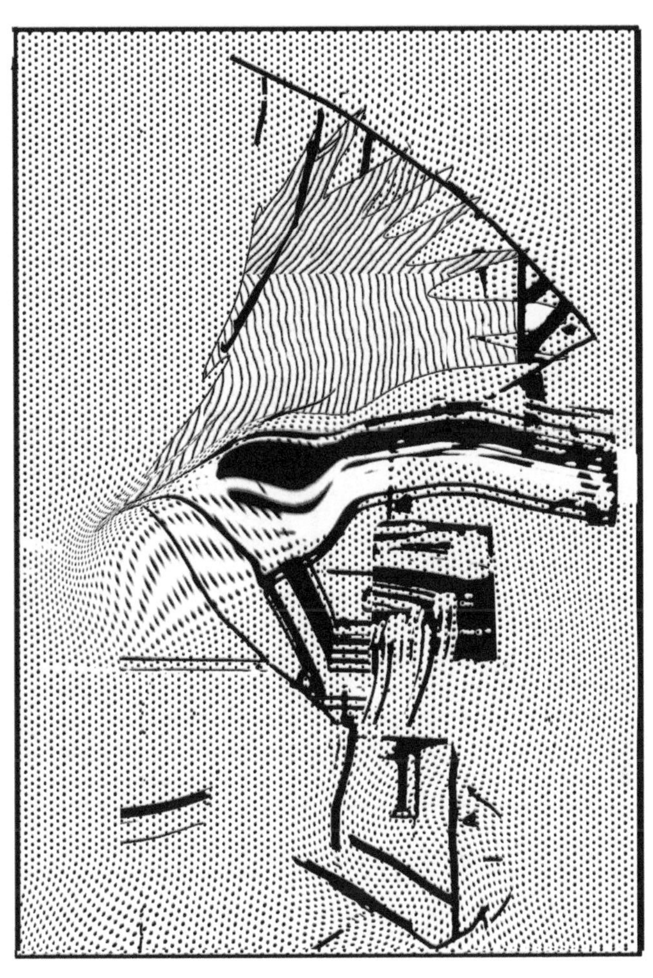

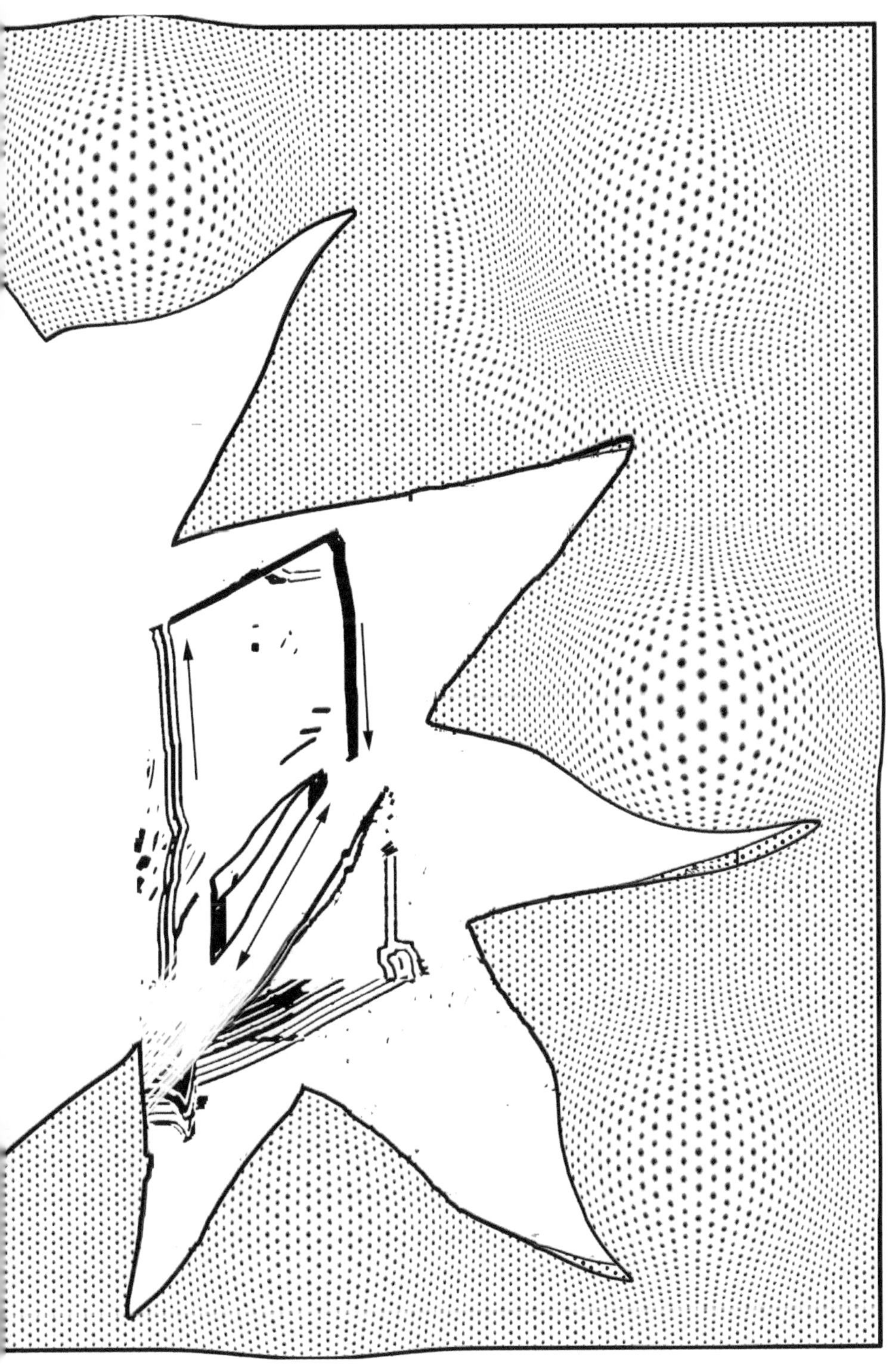

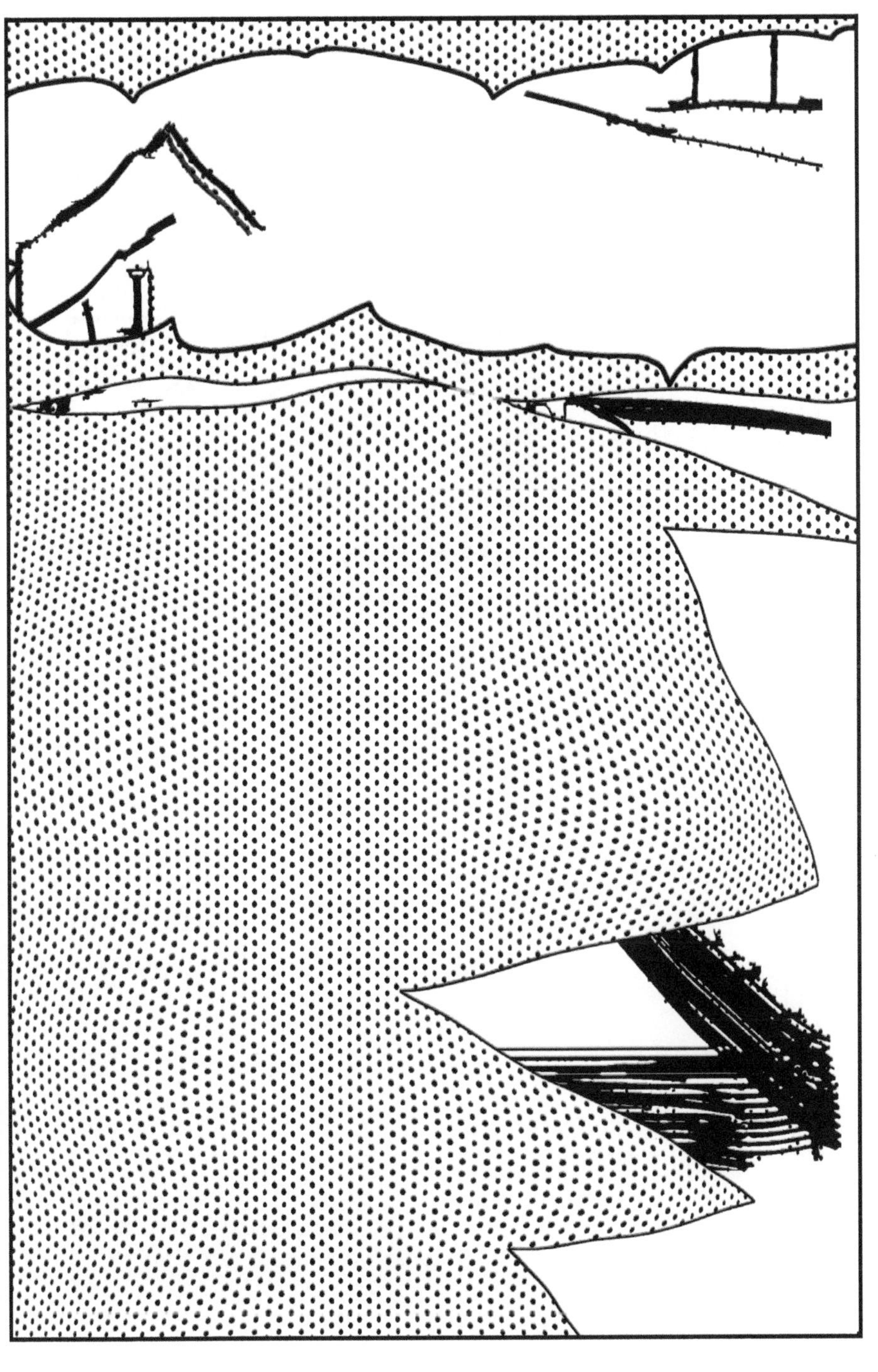

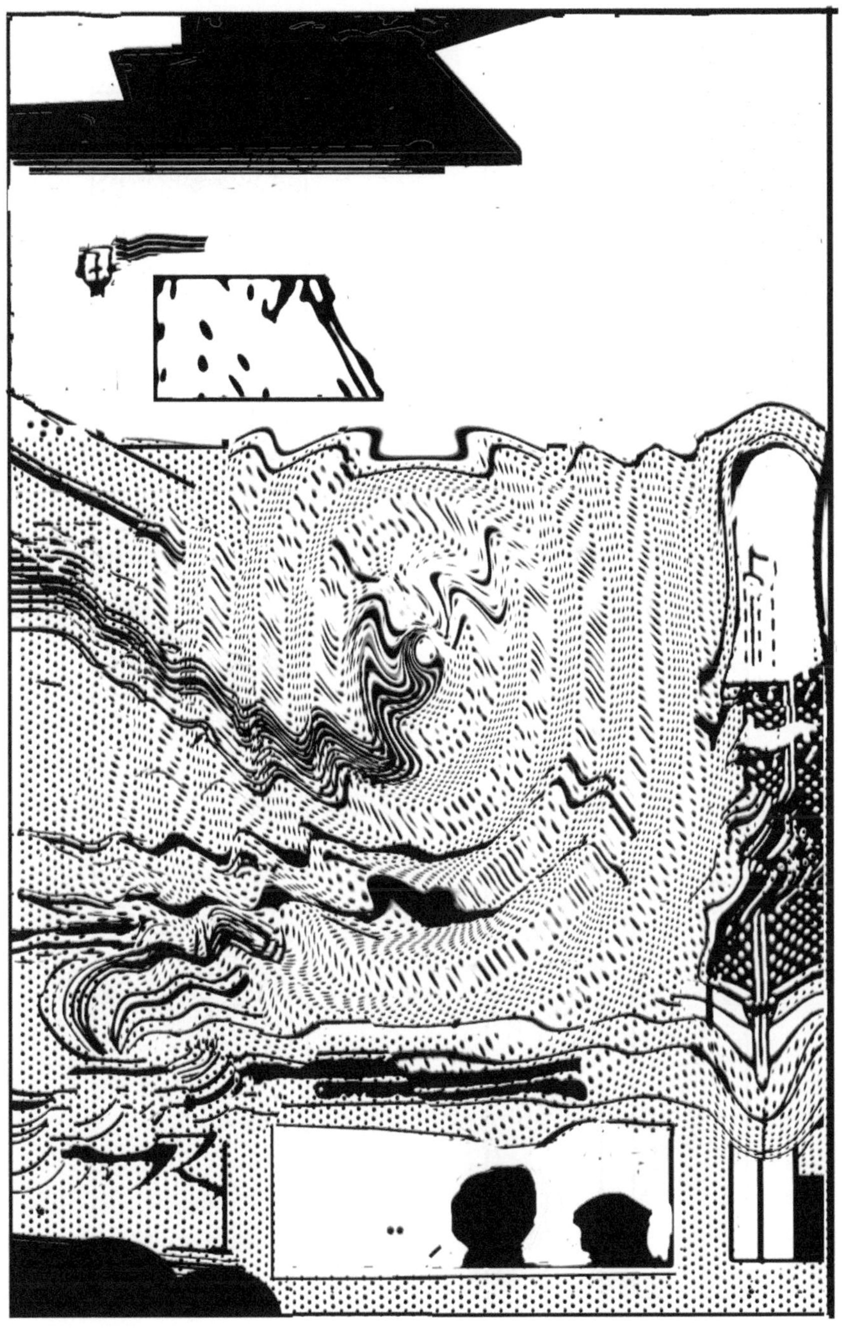

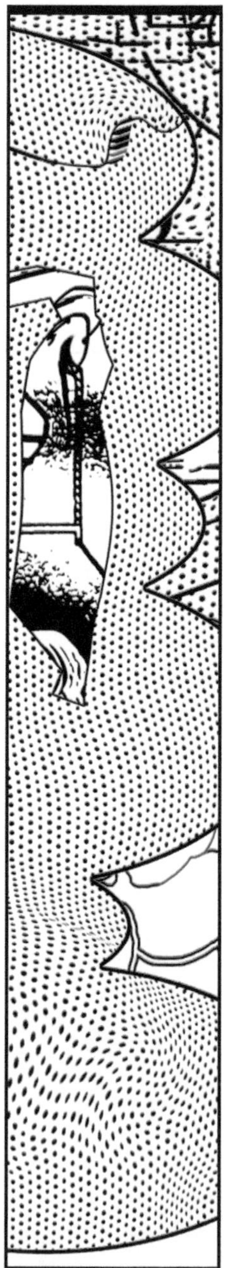

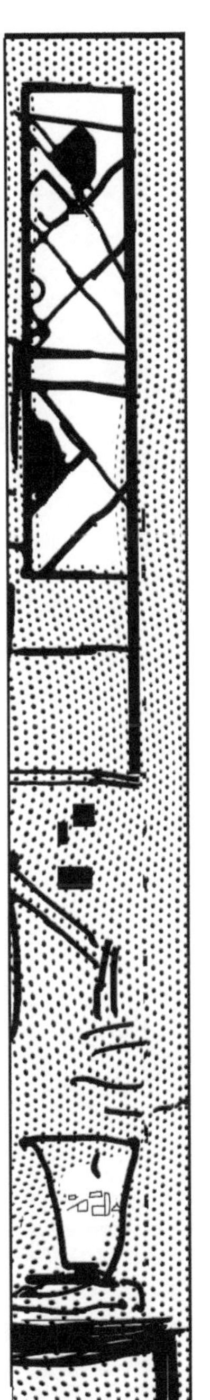

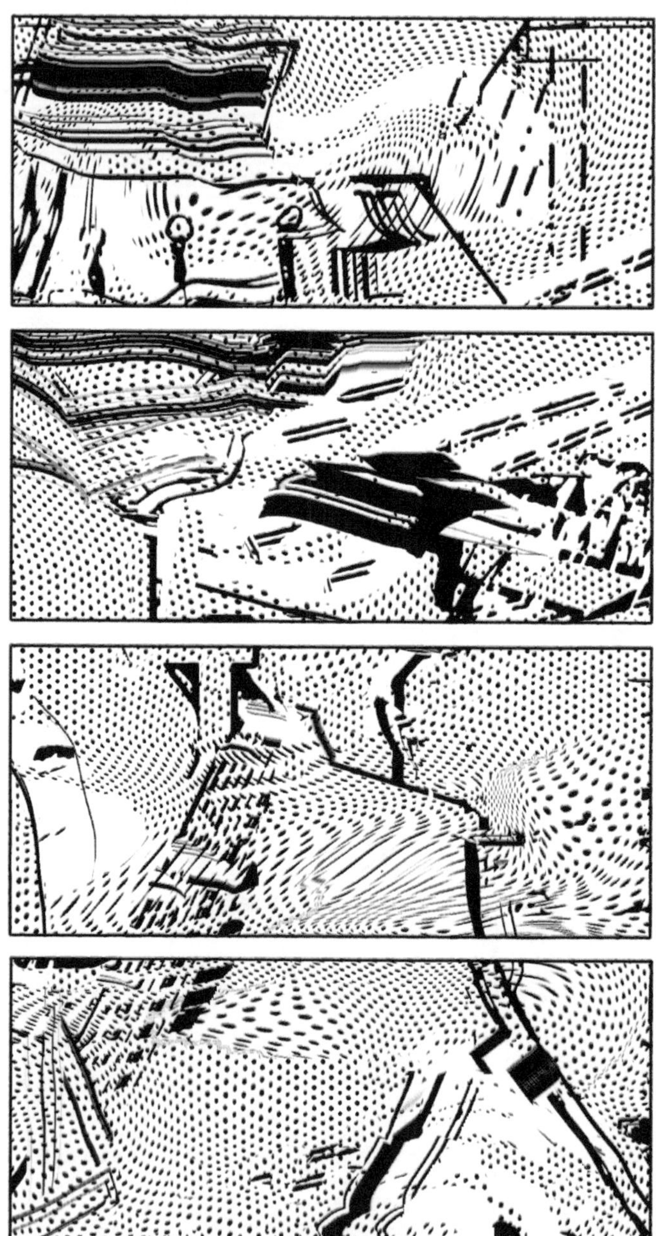

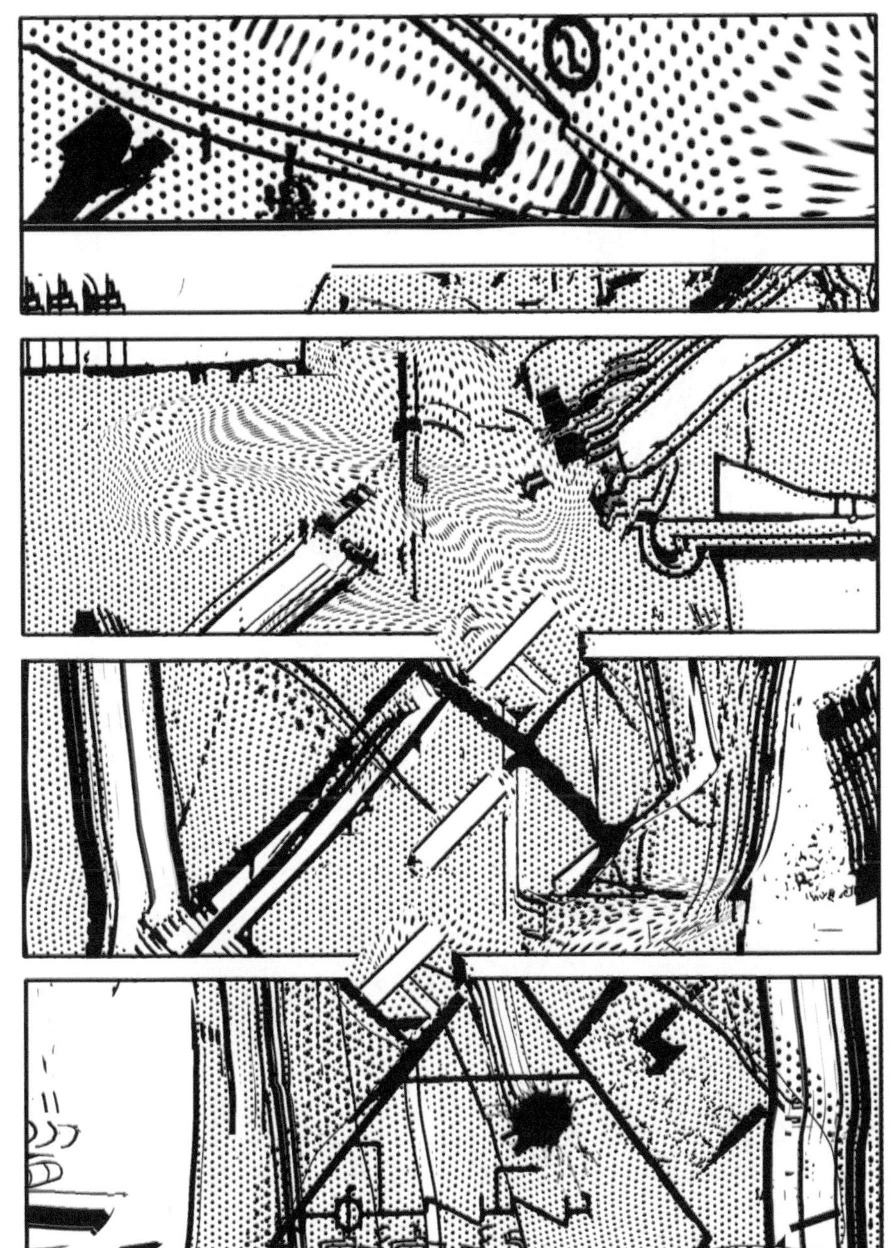

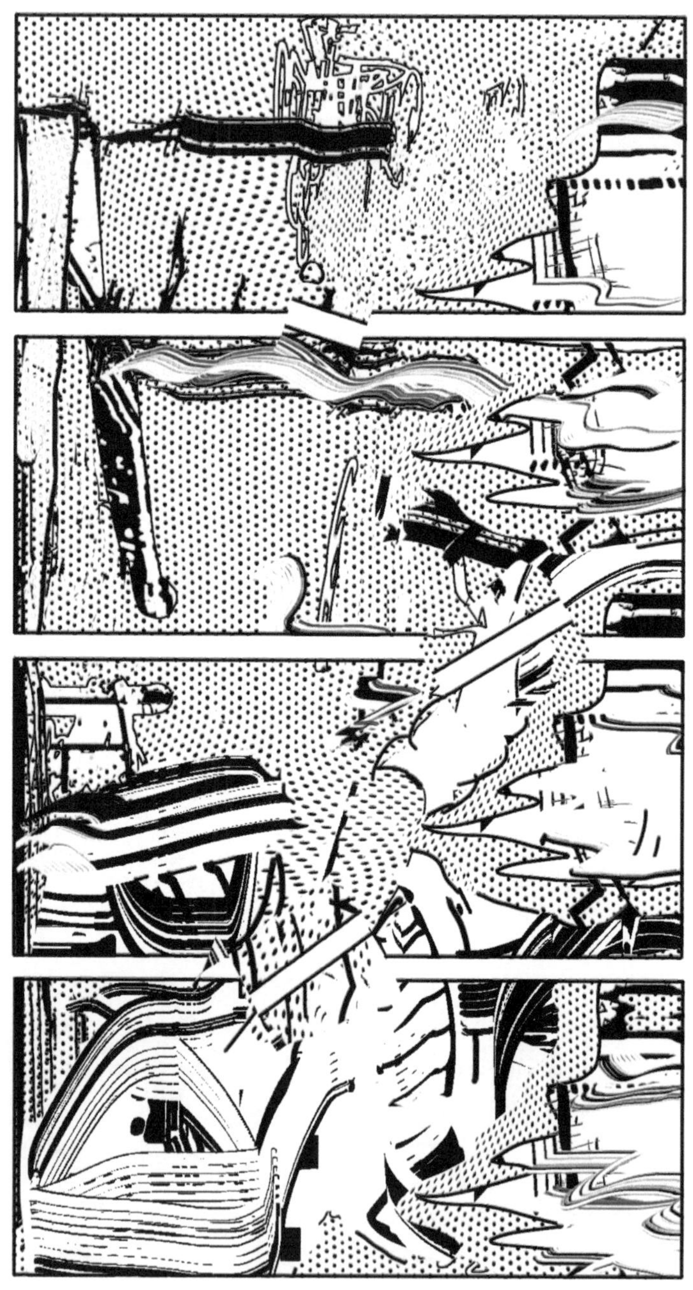

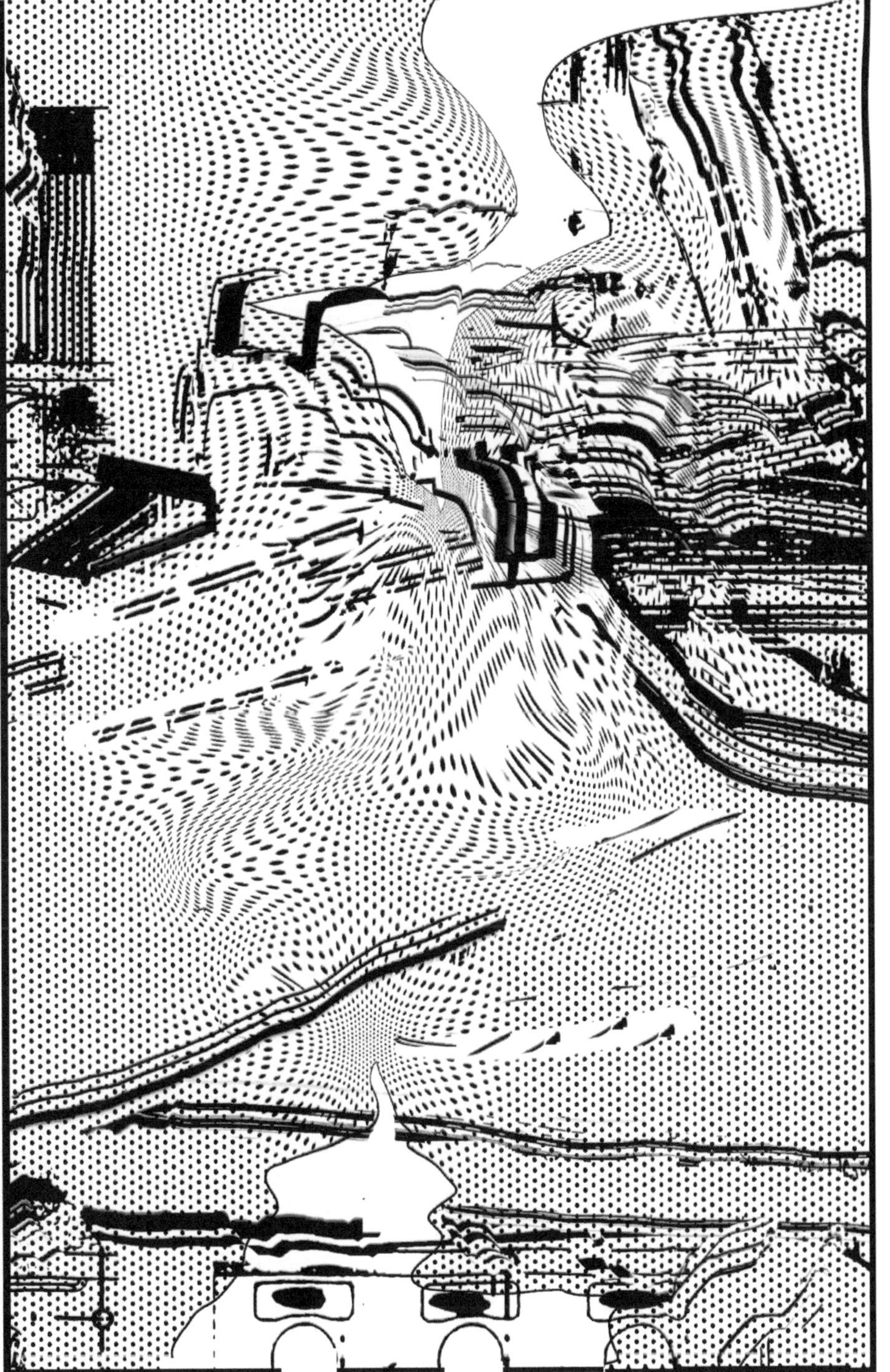

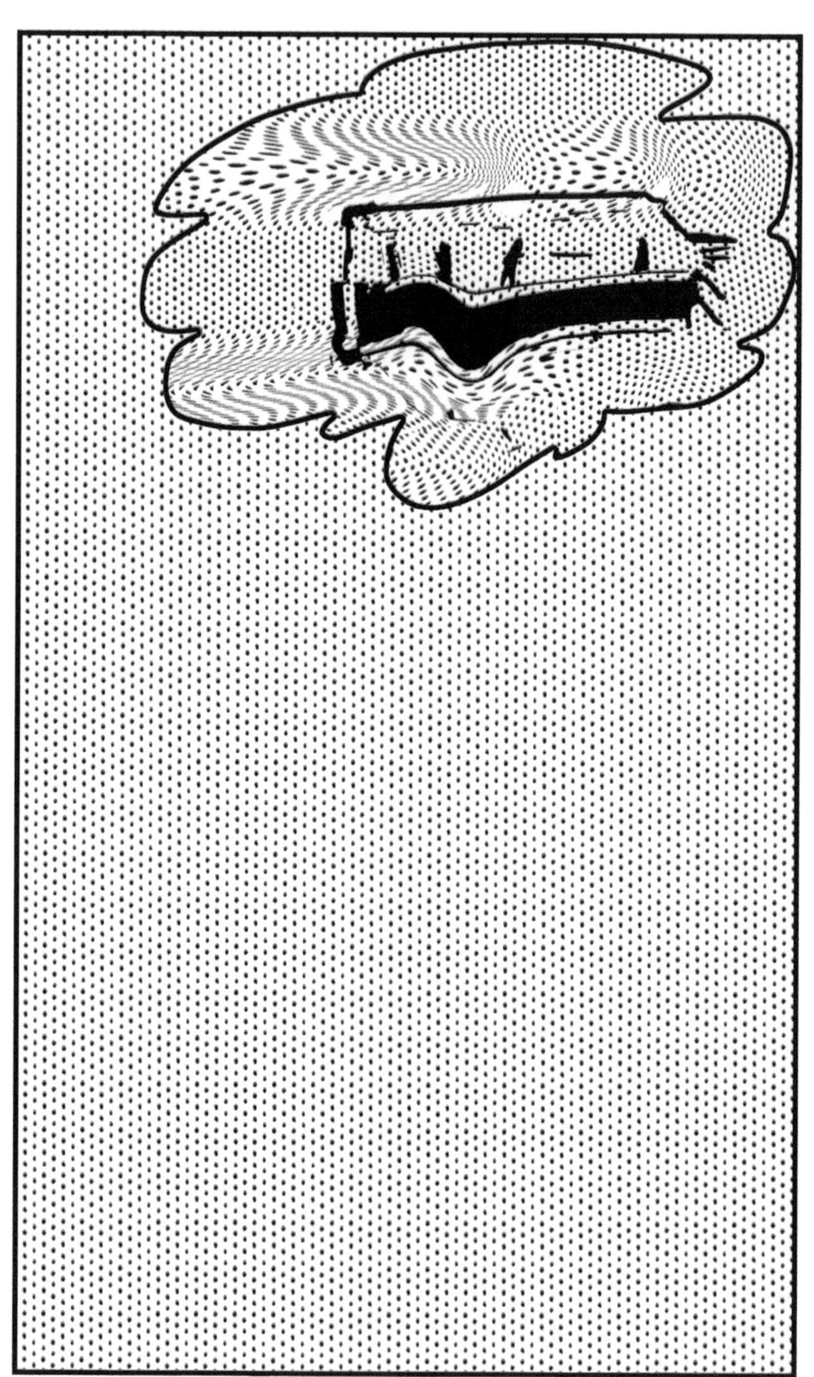

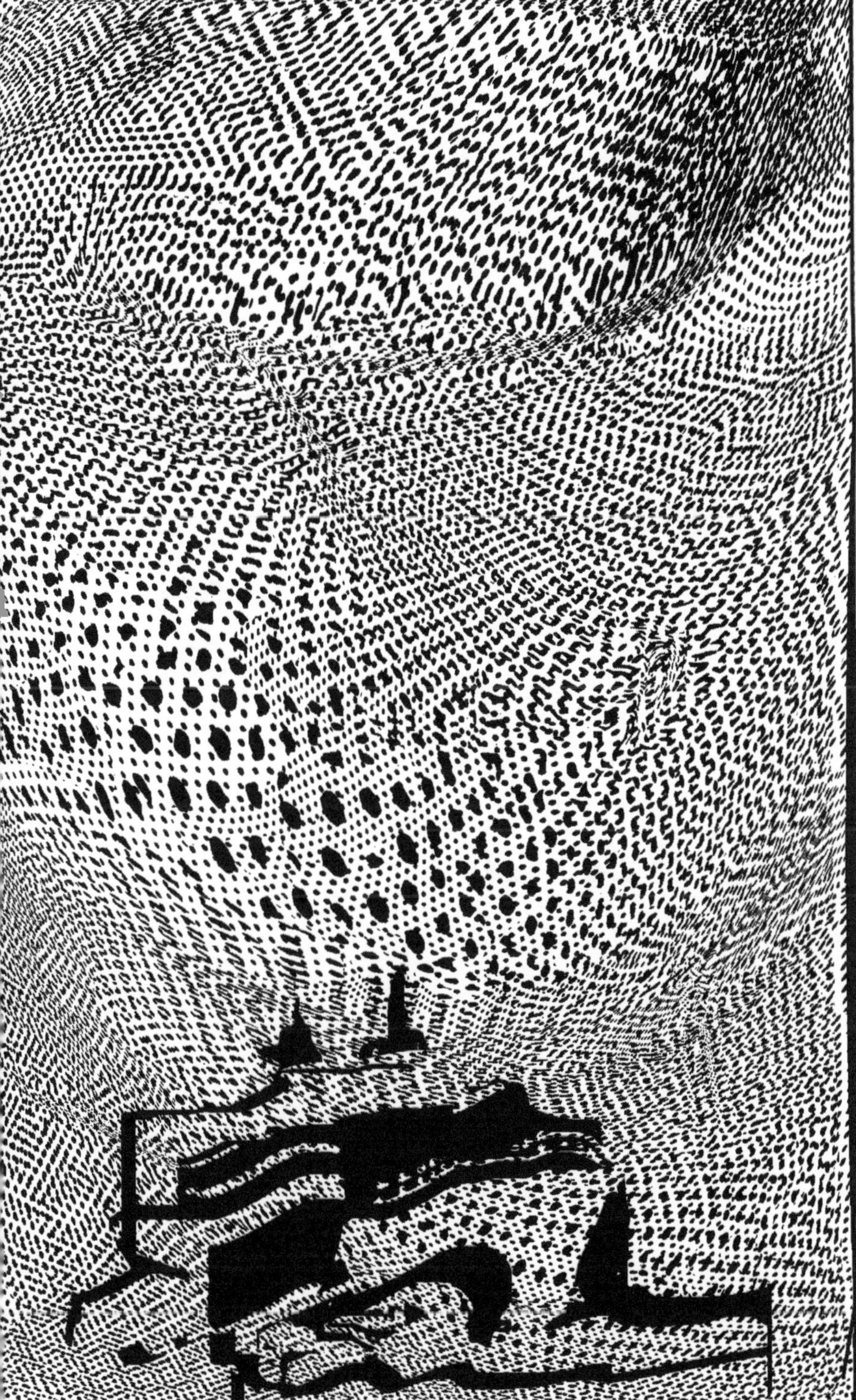

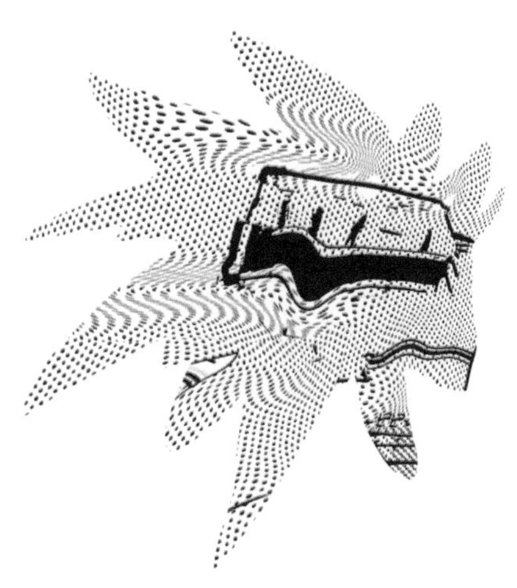

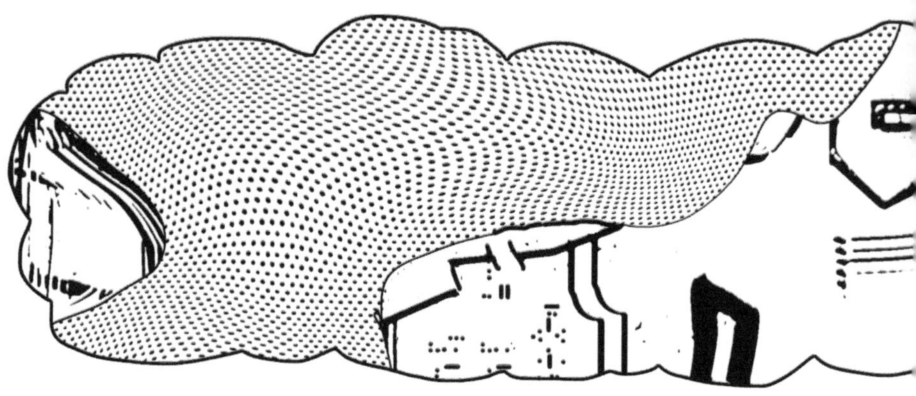

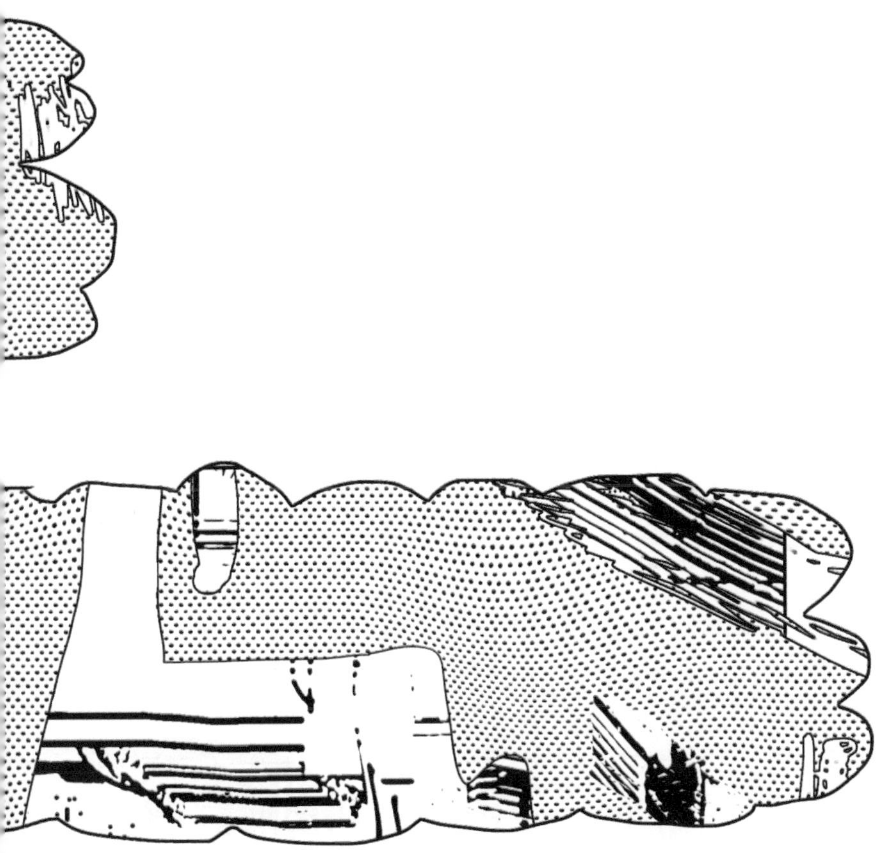

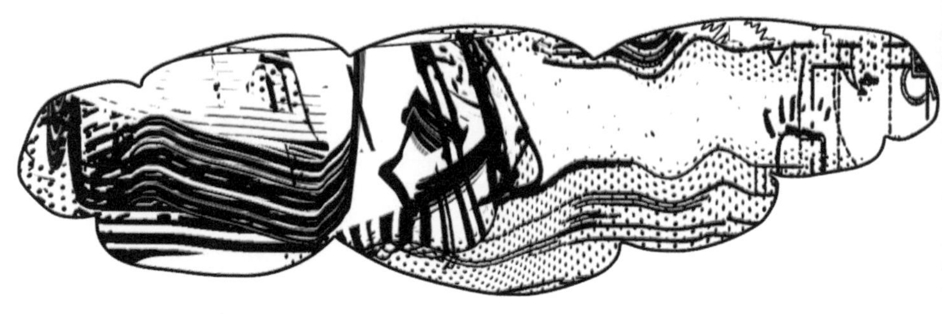

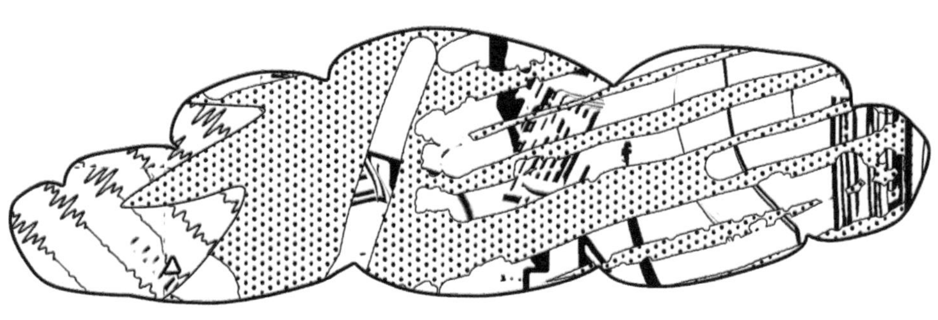

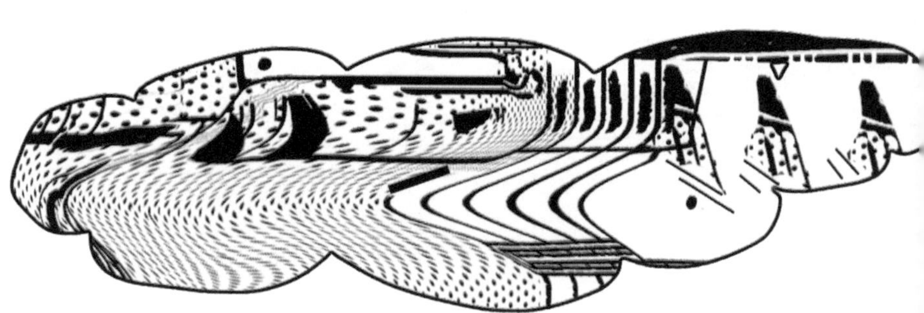

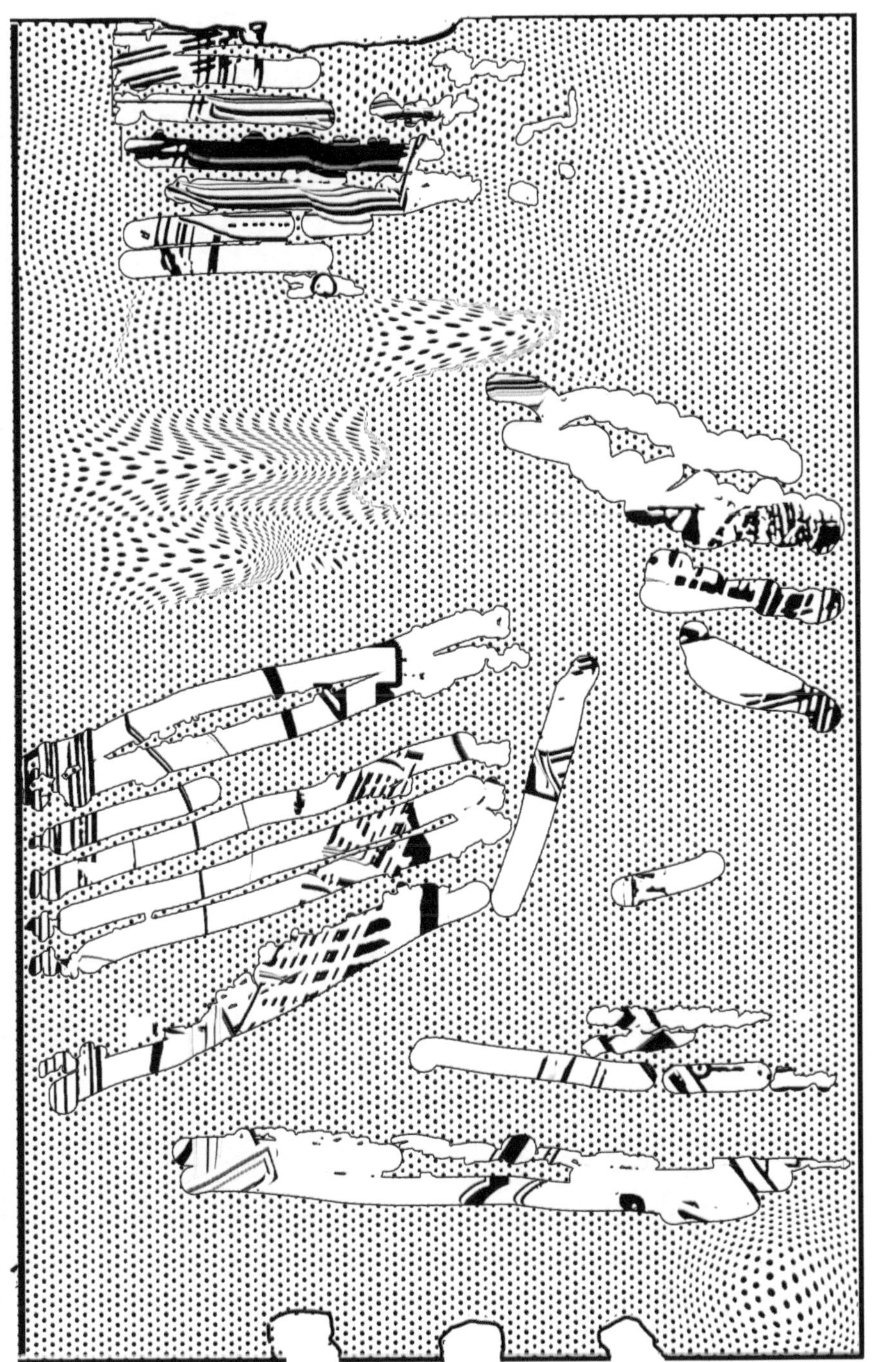

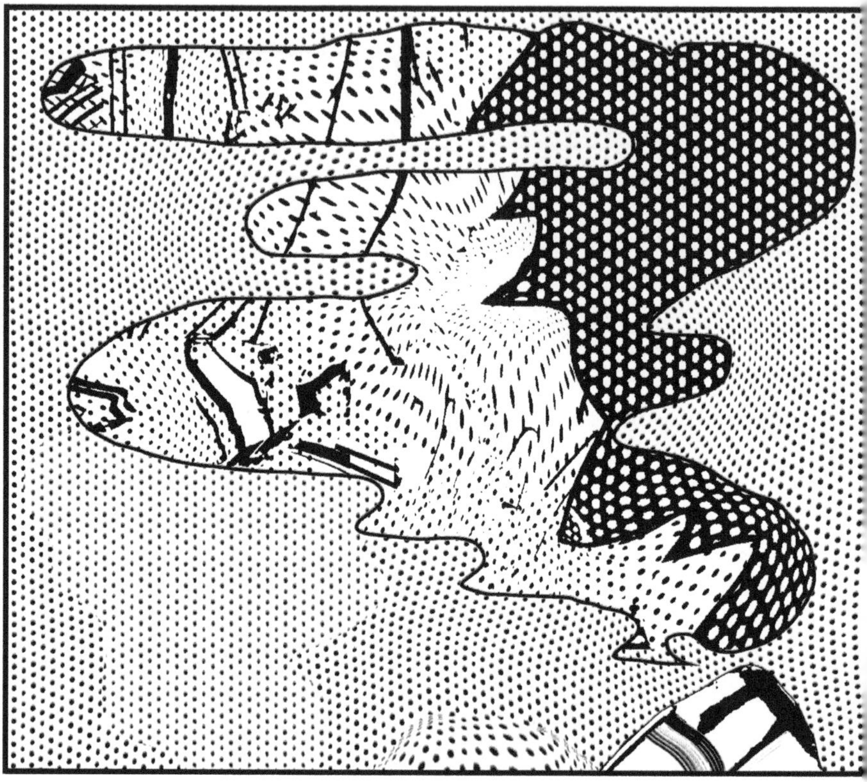

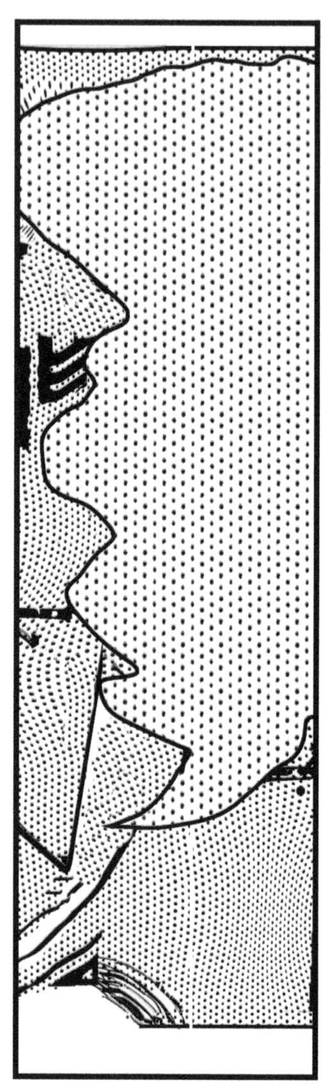

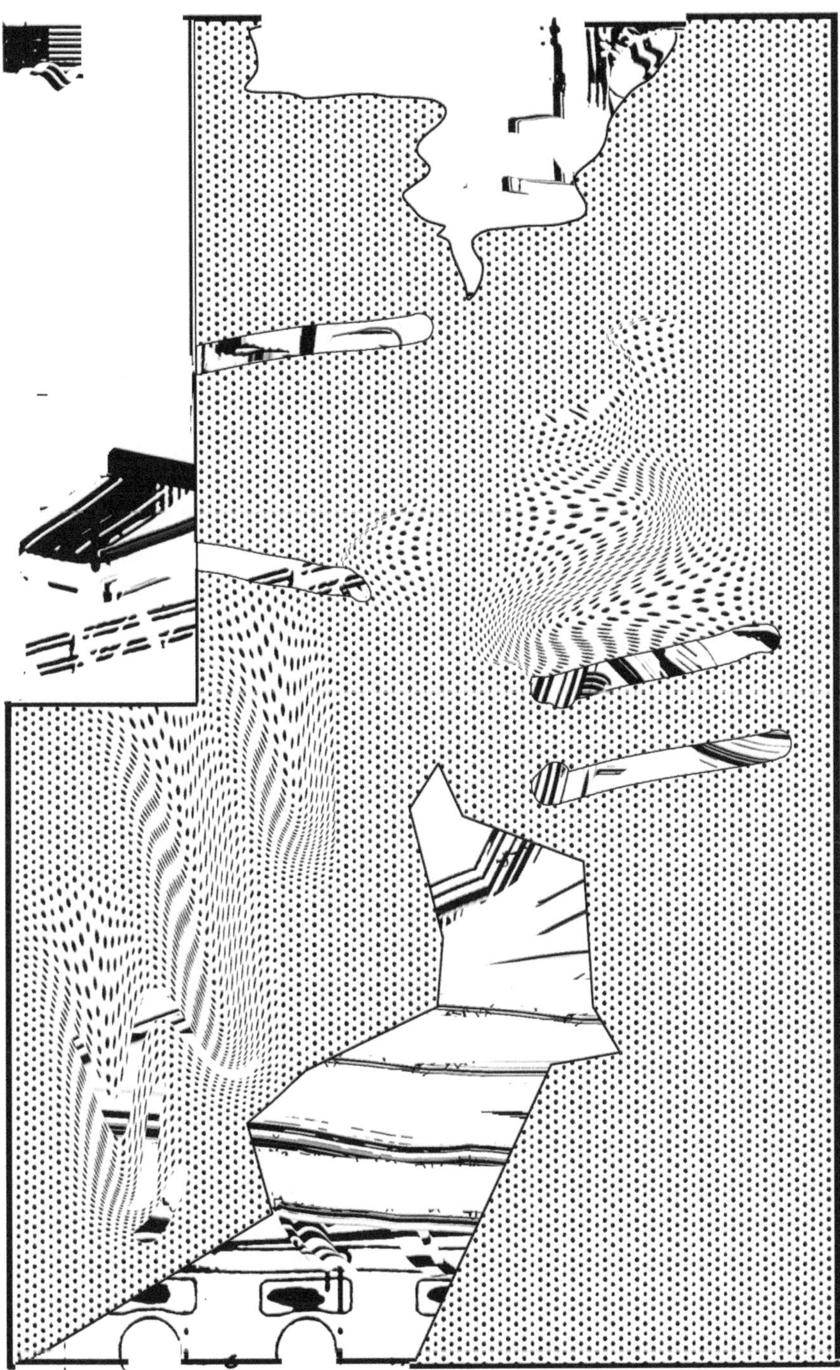

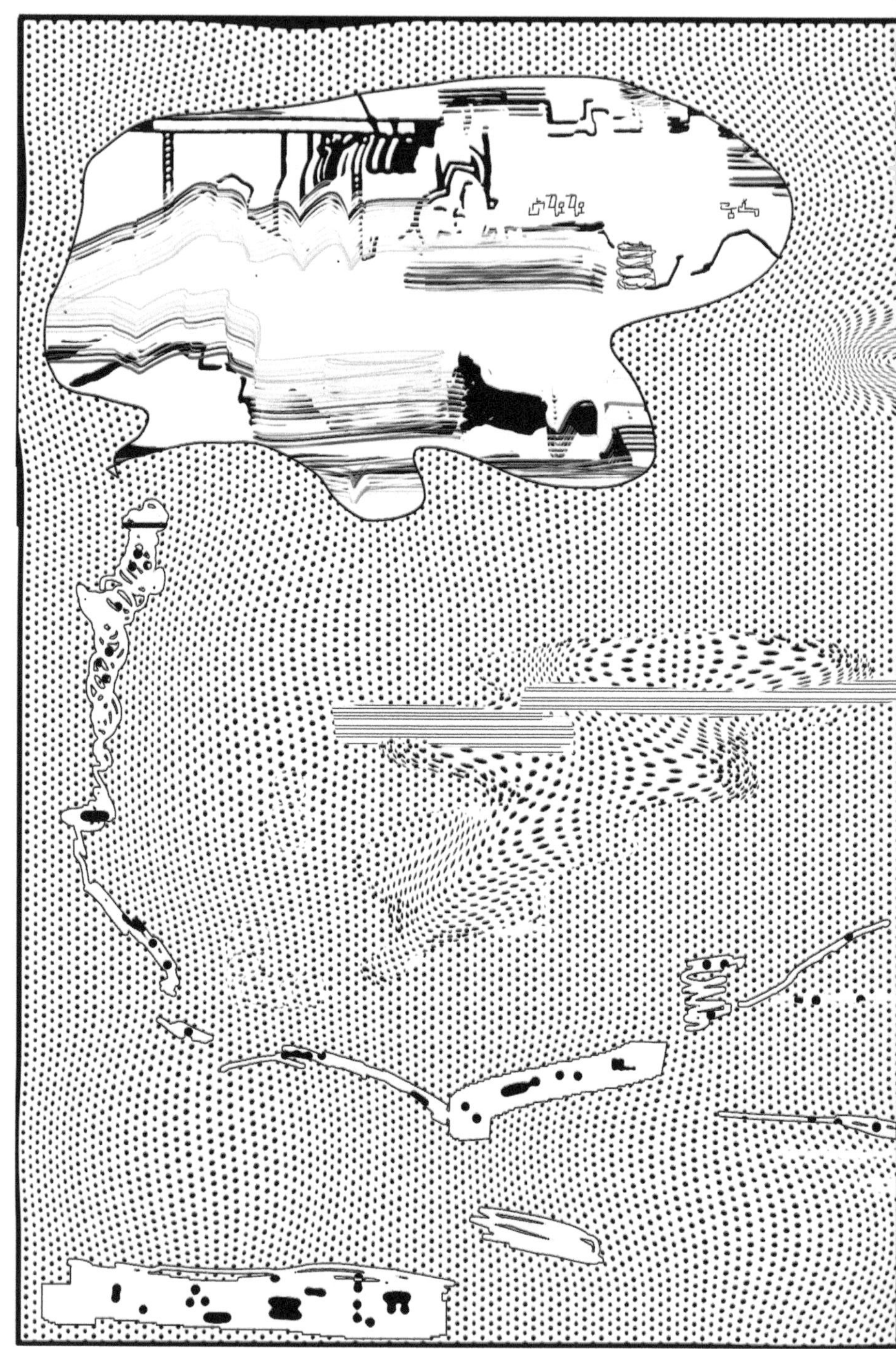

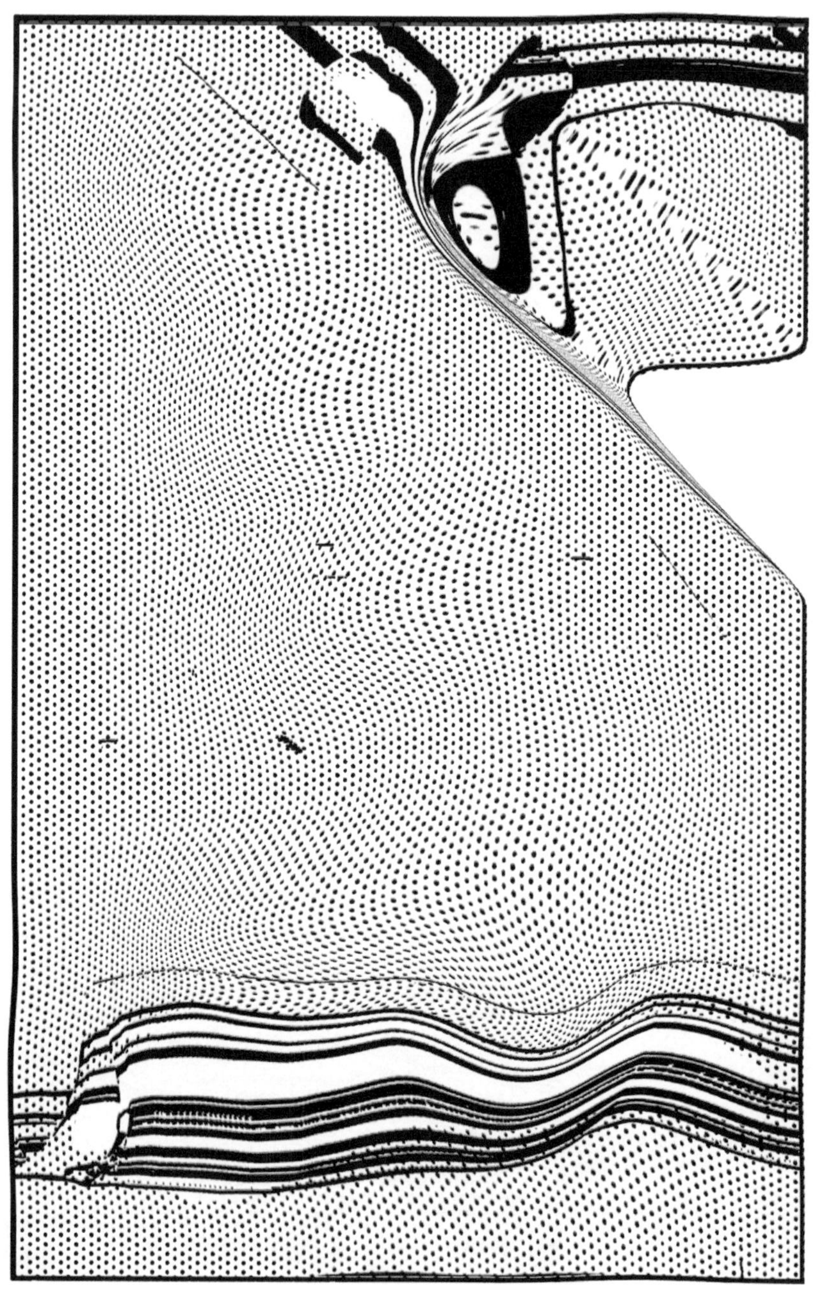

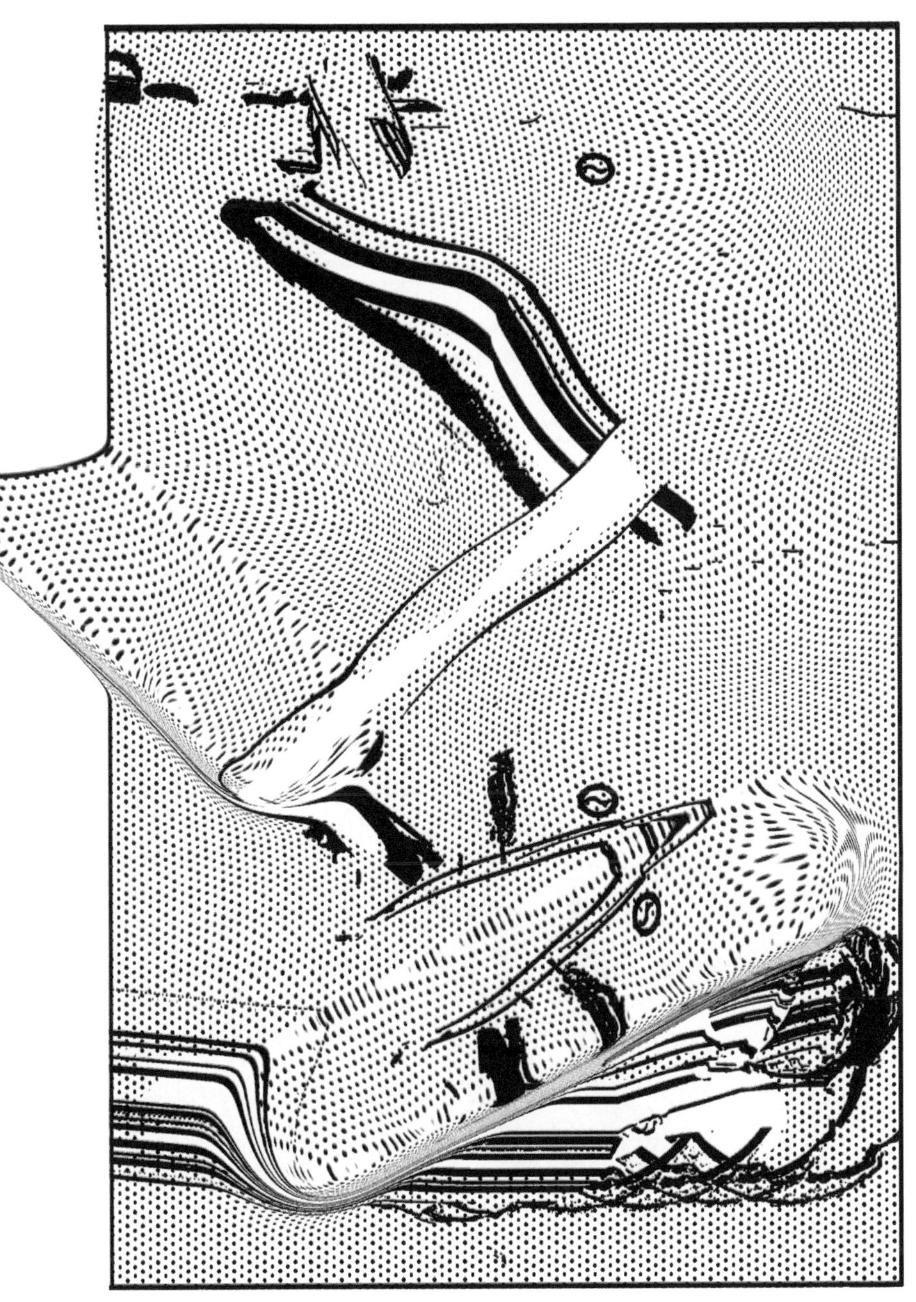

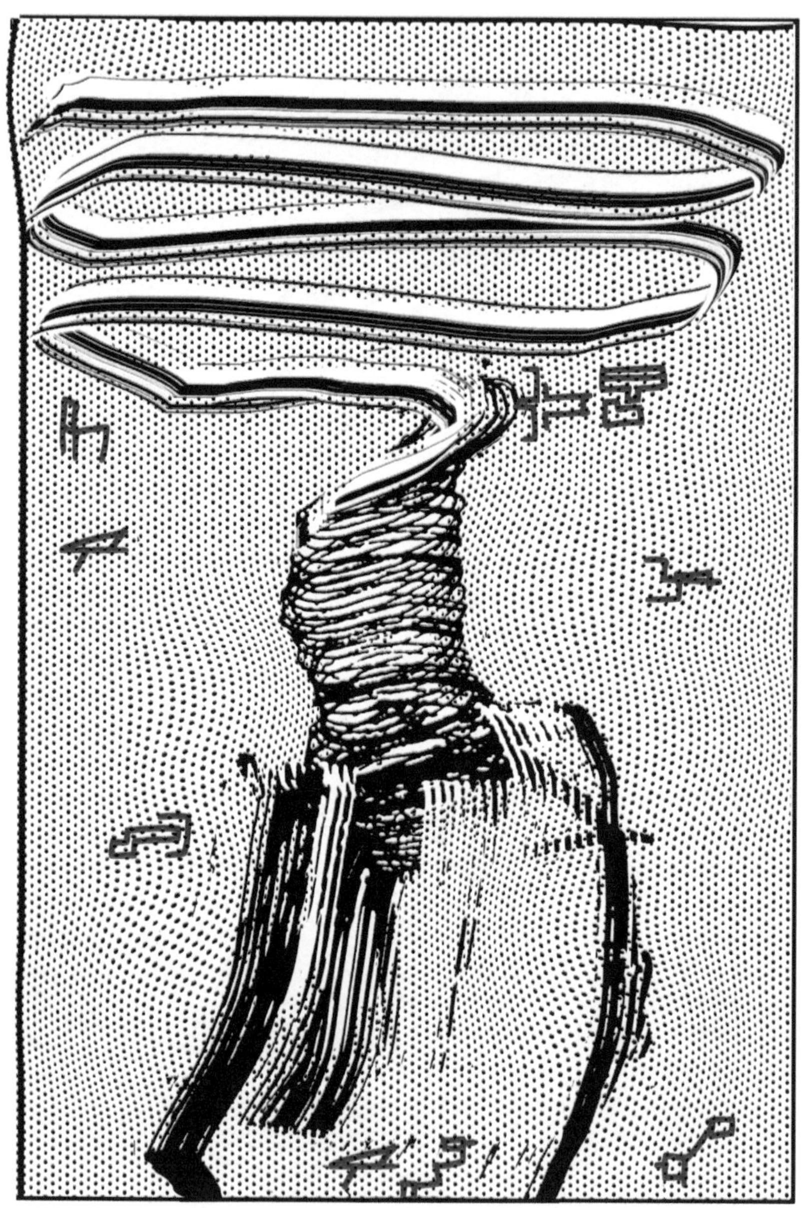

www.ingramcontent.com/pod-product-compliance
Ingram Content Group UK Ltd.
Pitfield, Milton Keynes, MK11 3LW, UK
UKHW041834200726
13854UKWH00003BA/1123